# ELENA'S INHERITANCE

A.A. VIVIAN

# *Table of contents*

## *CHAPTER ONE*

On a chilly winter evening, when Mr Ryan got home from work, his house was almost empty; he thought maybe someone broke in and stole their things. So, he called out to his wife. “Anna, Anna, are you okay, did someone break in?”
He did not get any response, so he rushed to his bedroom and noticed that his wife’s belongings were gone. Then he realised that his new wife had left him. He stood for some minutes while he tried to figure out what he did wrong. Their marriage was only 4 months old. they met in church for the first time in their little town before their parents arranged their marriage.

He picked up the telephone and called his wife’s parents. His mother in-law answered. “Hello...?”

"Good evening, Mrs Edwin. It is me, Ryan."

"Oh... Mr Ryan. Good evening to you."

"I am calling to ask if you've seen or heard from Anna."

"No, I have not. Where could she have gone?"

"I do not know, ma'am. Her things are missing. I think she has left me," he said.

"Oh my God, did you fight with her?" Mrs Edwin asked.

"No, we did not fight. She looked happy this morning before I left for work. I do not know what might have happened... but please let me know if she calls you."

"Okay, I will," Mrs Edwin said, and then she hung up.

Anna moved out from the house because she never loved Mr Ryan, but she was in love with a man from a nearby town, whom she met when she was visiting her brother.

Two months have passed, and Mr Ryan was yet to hear from his wife. He never stopped calling his wife's parents to know if they have heard from Anna, but his in-laws could not bring themselves to tell Mr Ryan that their daughter has already moved on. Ryan wanted closure; he wanted an explanation but after all his effort he started giving up. One day Mr Ryan got back from work, but before entering his house he decided to check the letter box. To his surprise, there were three envelopes in the box; he took them with him inside without checking what they were. He put the envelopes on his dining table and forgot about them.

Early morning of the fifth day, Mr Ryan woke up, and he headed to the kitchen to make coffee for himself like he does every other morning. After he made the coffee, he sat down, and he was about to take a sip when he noticed the edges of some white envelopes slightly under some newspapers. He stretched his hand to lift the newspapers and collected the envelopes; he opened the first two and they were his electricity bills that he needed to pay. So, he opened the last one and it was a divorce letter from his wife. After he read it, he immediately became sad and confused, even though he already knew his wife did not want to be with him anymore. But Mr Ryan had no idea why she left the way she did and where she was living.

That same morning. Mr Ryan put on his clothes and headed to the home of Anna's parents with the divorce letter, without informing them that he was coming. When he arrived, he packed his motorcycle at the front yard, and he walked his way to the wooden door in front of the house and he pressed the bell.

"Who is there? Please hold on, I am coming, Mrs Edwin said from the sitting room as she headed towards the door. When she opened the door, she saw Mr Ryan.

"Good morning, Mrs Edwin."

"Good morning to you, Mr Ryan. Why are you here this early morning and you did not inform us you were coming? Come in... come inside, it is cold," she said while directing Mr Ryan to the sitting room where Mr Edwin was.

"Please make yourself comfortable," said Mrs Edwin.

"Thank you, good morning, Mr Edwin. I apologise for not informing you before coming."

"Morning, Ryan, it's alright, you are welcome at any time, is everything okay?" said Mr Edwin.

"I received this letter a few days ago and I forgot to open it; this is a divorce letter from Anna," he said while showing the letter to Anna's parents.

"We are so sorry, Mr Ryan. A couple of weeks before Anna moved out from your house, she had told us that she was not in love with you, and she could not pretend anymore. We spoke to her and gave her some advice, but we did not know that she was actually going to leave you. And she only visited us two times since she left you. I know we should have told you about her visit, but we thought maybe she would return to you. We are sorry, Mr Ryan. I know we have hurt you," said Mrs Edwin.

"It is okay, Mrs Edwin. I knew she never loved me. but please whenever you hear from her again, let her know that I will sign the divorce paper so she can be legally free," Ryan said. A couple of minutes later he left.

On his way home, while he was riding his motorcycle, he started to cry. Mr Ryan cried because he really loved Anna. When he got home, he rushed inside the house, took his working bag, and headed to work because he was already running late.

Three years later after their divorce was finalised. Mr Ryan bought a farm in the neighbouring town where he grew up, and he relocated there, where he rears sheep and pigs. Mr Ryan excelled in ranching of his livestock, and he was known throughout the town and in other nearby towns. Anna was Mr Ryan's neighbour, and they lived a couple of miles away from each other. But Mr Ryan did not know that Anna, his ex-wife lives in the same town with him.

One evening when Mr Ryan was returning home from the nearby town with his truck full of pigs that he just purchased, he came across a man and a pregnant woman that was stranded on the side of the road. He could not just pass them because it was dark already and he knew that they might not get another opportunity for help, so he stopped his truck to ask the couple where they were headed and if they needed any help.

"Hello, do you need any help?" Mr Ryan asked.

"Yes please, our car broke down and we live in this town," the man said.

"Alright, get in with your partner. I can drop you off, I live in this town too," said Mr Ryan.

"Ah yes, we know you Mr Ryan, everybody knows you in this town," he said while he called out for his partner. "Anna, come get in, it's Mr Ryan."

When Anna heard the name Mr Ryan, she was shocked and at that moment she felt nothing but shame. They would have walked home but because Anna was heavily pregnant, she could not walk for long, so they needed help. She walked closer to the truck, and said,

"Thank you, Mr Ryan, for helping us."

Ryan looked at her in disbelief, and he hesitated to respond to her. Anna and her partner got in, and some minutes later they arrived at their house. They got down and thanked Mr Ryan for his kindness; as they walked away, Mr Ryan could not help but to look at Anna one more time before he left.

When Mr Ryan got home, he could not believe who he just saw and at the same time he was happy for her.

There was a woman named Elena from the town where Mr Ryan goes to buy his livestock. Elena was a single parent, and she was from the Gilbert family. which was one of the Elite in their town. She had two brothers, Erik was the oldest and Henry was the last child of the family, and Elena was the middle child and was also the odd one out of the family. Her family thinks of her as a disgrace for refusing to marry into an eligible family and having a child out of wedlock. Elena was different from her siblings despite coming from a rich family. But she had one friend named Kate, who understood and supported every decision she made. She was also there when Elena's family made her an outcast. Kate was a tailor, and she had a fashion shop where she sells handmade clothing.

Many years ago, before Elena had her daughter, she and Kate visited a vineyard and, on their way back home, they came across a market and walked to a particular shop that sells beautiful hair clips and scarfs, so they decided to buy some for themselves. While they were trying different hair clips, Elena picked a pink hair clip and said to Kate, "I think this will look good on me."

"It's beautiful but you don't like pink," Kate responded,

"Yeah, I know but it's very pretty," she said. While she was searching for a different colour, she saw a purple butterfly hair clip; she picked it up and was looking at it, and then heard a voice saying, "It will look good on you. It matches your dress." Elena looked back and with a warm smile she responded, "I was thinking of buying this, thanks anyways." the young man walked towards them and said, "Hi, I'm Patrick, and I am buying a gift for my mother, it's her birthday tomorrow."

"Oh, that's nice, I'm Elena and this is my friend Kate."

"Pleasure to meet you, where are you ladies from? You do not look like you are from this town," he said.

"No, we are from the neighbouring town," Kate replied. After they talked for some time.

"Kate, let's go, it's getting late," said Elena. They paid for what they got and said goodbye to Patrick. They got their bicycles and rode home.

A few days after their encounter with Patrick. Elena was sent an errand to the post office; on her way back, she walked past a building that was still in construction, filled with workers. Then she heard someone call her name.

"Elena, Elena!" She turned to the direction where the voice was coming from and noticed a man waving at her from the construction building, but she did not recognise him. While she stood there in confusion trying to figure out who the man was, Patrick hurried down from the building to say hello to Elena. When he got to where she was standing, "Hi, it's me Patrick, we met few days ago at the market," he said

"Oh yes, I remember. Hi, hi... I did not know it was you," Elena said

"We meet again, you are from this town, right?" Patrick said.

"Yes. what are you doing here?"

"I came here to work, I am a carpenter, as you can see," Patrick replied as he looked up to the building where there were other workers. They talked for a few minutes, and he made Elena smile a lot; she was all giggling as she talked to him.

"I will be working here for another three days," he said.

"Okay, then we shall meet again tomorrow," Elena said. They said their goodbyes, she left, and Patrick returned to his work.

The next day, Elena prepared some fruits and placed them in a little basket; she took it with her and headed to where Patrick works. When she arrived, Patrick was outside the building like he knew the exact time that Elena would arrive. When they saw each other, they smiled.

"Hello stranger, are you done working for today?" Elena said.

"Yes beautiful, I am done for the day," he said as he gave Elena a warm smile.

They sat beside the short fence surrounding the building where Patrick works. They talked and ate the fruit Elena brought. It was a beautiful evening and after some time, Elena stood up and said,

"I have to go now."

"Okay, sure I will walk with you." He walks Elena a few blocks to her house.

"You can go back now," she said anxiously while she kept looking around.

"Alright, can we meet tomorrow?"

"Yes, I will meet you tomorrow, same time, goodbye Patrick," she replied while she hurried to her house.

"Goodbye Elena," he said, and he stood for some time as he watched her go.

Patrick and Elena grew fond of each other, they continued to see each other even after Patrick stopped working in her town. They would meet every third day of the week at the stream that divides their town; they eat, talk, and laugh. They were in love, but Elena knew that her family will never accept Patrick, but she could not tell him because she knew it will break his heart. But the only person who knew about them was Kate.

Patrick was poor, and he lived with his sick mother. His father died when he was only two-years-old. He dropped out from school because his mother could not pay his tuition fee, so he learnt carpentry to take care of his mother. He was already a grown man when he met Elena and he wanted to make her his bride. So, he told his mother about Elena, the maiden he spent his time with. His mother was excited to meet Elena, the girl who captured her son's heart.

On the third day of that week, Patrick visited the stream and waited for Elena for over an hour. He thought Elena was not coming, immediately he wanted to return home, but then he heard his name.

He turned and saw it was Elena; he ran and hugged her and said, “I thought you weren't coming today.”

“I am sorry. I had to run some errands for my mother. I apologise for keeping you waiting.”

“It is all right. I did not wait very long,” he said. They sat by the stream and were talking about their desire to always be with each other. Then Patrick suddenly said,

“My mother wants to meet you; I told her about you.” Elena was shocked and she hesitated before responding.

“Really, that would be nice. I would love to meet her too but not today.”

“Okay, maybe some other time,” Patrick said. They continued enjoying each other’s company, and after a short time, he walked Elena to her town. But he noticed that he was never allowed to walk to the front of Elena’s house. They said goodbye and he left.

When Elena got inside the house, she saw her father drinking tea with a guest. She did not think much of it, she said hello to her father and the guest and walked straight into her room. A few minutes later, she heard a knock on her door. “Come in,” she said.

“Were you out with Kate?” Mrs Gilbert asked.

“Yes, mother,” Elena responded. She lied about being with Kate when she was actually with Patrick.

“I thought so. Elena, you are due for marriage, all your age group are already married.”

“Mother, I will get married when the time comes.”

"When the time comes? When will that be?" Mrs Gilbert said in an angry tone, and she continued to say,

"Did you see the man drinking tea with your father? He has come to ask for your hand in marriage."

"What? That old man?" Elena said, disgusted. "No, no mother, I will not marry him. He is too old."

"How do you mean old? He is one of the most eligible bachelors in our town, and he owns a lot of properties too. He is rich Elena, he is wealthy," Mrs Gilbert said in persuasion.

"Mother, I want to marry for love not money," Elena said.

"He can take care of you. and he promised to give us his bakery and the land beside the post office as a token of appreciation. But only if you accept him."

"No, mother. I decline his proposal, and besides, I am in love with someone else," Elena said.

"What? Who? What family is he from? Does he have inheritance?" Mrs Gilbert asked.

"No, mother, he is not from our town. His name is Patrick, and he is a carpenter."

"What? Mrs Gilbert said angrily. "A carpenter?"

"Mother, he is a good man; he is kind, he takes care of his mother and I want to be with him."

"That cannot happen, you are the only daughter of our family. Do not bring disgrace to this family. I beg you, Elena."

"I love Patrick and I want to be with him."

"A carpenter as a son-in-law? That will never happen," Mrs Gilbert said angrily as she stormed out from Elena's room. Elena was left in confusion. She was already in love with Patrick, even though she knew her family would never accept him.

## *CHAPTER TWO*

On the third day of the next week, Elena got dressed to go see Patrick. She entered her mother's kitchen and took some fruit as usual and headed out. When she got to the stream, she sat down to wait for Patrick, and in a moment, she started to think out loud without realising and did not notice when Patrick got to where she was.

"Elena, are you okay?" said Patrick as he touched her on the left shoulder.

"Oh my God. Patrick, you scared me, when did you get here?"

"Not long, what are you thinking about? You were lost in thought. Is everything all right?"

"I am alright, I'm just tired."

"Are you sure?"

"Yes, I'm sure," she said with a not convincing smile on her face. "I missed you."

"I missed you too, my dearest," he replied.

They sat and enjoyed each other's company as usual. "Would you like us to go see my mother today?" Patrick said in excitement.

"Today? I would love to but er... it is getting late; I need to go home now. I will go with you when we meet again next week, I promise," she said.

"You want to go home now?" he asked.

"Yes now. I am very tired, Patrick, and I do not feel too good," Elena said.

"Okay, next week it is. I will walk you home," he said.

He held her hand While they were walking until they got near Elena's house. "I will see you next week," said Elena.

"Okay, goodbye Elena."

"Goodbye Patrick," she said as she hurried to her house.

Patrick turned and was walking back home. A moment later, while he was still on his way home, a car stopped in front of him. A man with a walking stick came out from the back seat and walked his way to Patrick.

"Are you Patrick?" the man asked.

"Yes, I am Patrick. Who is asking?"

"I am Elena's father."

"Oh, good evening, sir. I did not recognise you," Patrick said.

"How could you? We have never met," Mr Gilbert said in disgust.

"Yes, you are right sir."

"I see you walked Elena home; did she tell you that she is getting married very soon?"

Patrick was shocked to hear that news from Elena's father. He did not know what to say so he kept quiet.

"Leave Elena alone, now that I am asking politely. What do you have to offer her? She is my only daughter, and she must marry a rich man from a well-known family."

Patrick still could not say a word while he listened quietly to everything Mr Gilbert had to say. After Mr Gilbert finished talking, he turned to walk back to his car when he heard Patrick saying,

"I love her. I love Elena and I intend to make her my wife."

Without responding, Mr Gilbert entered his car and left. Patrick continued his journey back home, but he was not himself, and he kept thinking maybe that was the reason why Elena kept hesitating to meet his mother.

With too many problems going on in Elena's home for refusing to marry a rich man, Patrick and Elena met at the stream that week.

"Patrick, I am worried. My family is against me; they want me to marry a rich man, so I can bring more wealth to the family," Elena said.

"I know. Your father made it clear to me the last time I accompanied you home."

"What? You spoke to my father? How did he recognise you? I am sorry, Patrick," she said.

"You do not have to apologise... I just... wish I were rich." He then took a deep breath.

"Do not say that. It is you I want, Patrick."

"Elena, would you marry me if I asked?"

"Of course, I will, you know I will," she said shyly. Patrick then picked a dried leaf stem and made it into the shape of a ring and placed it on Elena's finger and said, "Hold onto this. I will replace it with a real and better one someday."

After Elena collected the leaf ring from Patrick she stood up from where she was sitting and took Patrick's hand.

"Come with me, come home with me. I want to introduce you to my family as the man I want to marry."

"Wait, what?" Patrick said as Elena took him with her in a hurry.

They both arrived at the front of Elena's home. They stood outside for a few seconds and took a deep breath.

"Are we really doing this?" he asked.

"Yes, we are," she replied hastily. They walked inside the house holding each other's hands.

Mr Gilbert was reading a newspaper in the tearoom when Elena and Patrick walked in. Mr Gilbert recognized Patrick instantly and without hesitation he said, "Young man, what are you doing in my house?"

"Father, this is Patrick, the man I want to marry," Elena said without allowing Patrick to respond to her father's question.

"Marry? On whose blessing?" Mr Gilbert replied.

"Sir, I love your daughter. and I know that I am not financially stable right now, but I promise I will work hard, and I will take good care of her, I promise you this, sir. Please give us your blessing," Patrick said.

"Patrick or whatever your name is, get out of my house and I do not want to ever see you near my daughter again. I told you the last time we met that she was already betrothed to a rich man."

"Father, I cannot and will not marry that old man. Father, he is older than you," Elena said tearfully

"Stop crying Elena," Patrick said. and he wiped off the tears on Elena's face with his hand.

"Get out of my house!" Mr Gilbert continued to say but in a much-vexed tone this time.

Patrick walked out from the house with disappointment.

"Wait, wait for me Patrick," Elena said as she ran after him.

"Go back inside, please go back inside. I will never be accepted by your family," he said with tears dropping down his cheeks.

"I will see you next week," he said and he left hurriedly while Elena stood there in confusion.

After she could not see his back anymore, she stormed inside the house and started yelling at her father. "If I don't marry Patrick, I will not marry anyone else," she said.

"I will remove your name from the family registry if you go against my will," Mr Gilbert said as he continued to read his newspapers.

Elena was stunned to hear her father say that to her. She could not say any more words as she walked quietly into her room. She locked herself in her room for two days without food or water. And on the evening of the second day, she came out. Immediately when she opened the door, her mother rushed to her.

"Oh sweetheart, look at you, so lean. Why did you put yourself through this?"

"Mother, please stop talking. I am starving," she said faintly. "None of you cared to know if I was still alive."

"We knew you were alive, because we hear you cry, and there is food in the kitchen, eat as much as you can," Mrs Gilbert said.

Elena walked her way into the kitchen, took food and ate. After eating she got dressed, took her bicycle, and headed to Kate's house.

"Hello Elena, come sit with me. I have been spending all my free time making this embroidery. look, isn't it beautiful? I am making it for my little cousin," Kate said.

"Yes, it is very beautiful," Elena replied,

"I haven't seen you in so long. how have you been and why do you look so sad?" Kate asked as she dropped the embroidery needle and focused on Elena.

"I am not okay. My father has refused to let me marry Patrick. He threatened to remove my name from the family registry." Elena busted out crying.

"I am confused, I love Patrick, I love him," she said quietly.

"Oh Elena, it must be exceedingly difficult for you. I can only imagine. But why is your father against it? You love Patrick and he loves you; isn't that all that matters?

"My parents want me to marry an old man, so I can bring more wealth to the family."

"An old man, that is so sad, what are you going to do now?"

"I do not know; and I do not know how Patrick is faring. The last time I saw him, he was crying after my father sent him out, I have no idea of what to do." Elena said in confusion.

Kate sighed and said, "Do whatever you want to do, and I will be by your side. I will always be here for you Elena. I know you love Patrick so much and you love your family too, and whichever side you take, you will end up hurting the other. This is so frustrating."

"I know. I have thought about every possible way to make both sides happy, but I could not find one except...," Elena paused without finishing her statement.

"Except what?" Kate asked.

"Hmm... nothing. I was just thinking of running away."

"Running away? With Patrick? But if you run away, you will not get any inheritance from your family."

"Yes, I know. I am just thinking about it though." Elena spent some time with Kate, and they chatted for a while, then she returned home.

Elena and Patrick met again at their usual spot beside the stream.

"I missed you Patrick," she said.

"I missed you too. How are you, Elena?"

"I am okay. Patrick, I am sorry about what my father said to you."

"It is all right Elena, I have forgotten all about it. I was thinking about you, and I am sorry about how I walked away from you that day, I was just disappointed, and I hated the fact I was poor. Well... now I must work extremely hard if I am to make you my wife," he said.

After Elena and Patrick talked about the current issue they were facing, it was getting very dark, but Elena was not in a hurry to return home like she always does.

"Elena, it is getting very dark, I should walk you home," Patrick said.

"Walk with me," Elena said as she took Patrick's hand.

"Where are we going? This is not the direction to your home," he said.

"Shhh, I know," she said quietly.

She took Patrick into an empty mill that was close to the stream. "What are we doing here?" Patrick asked. Elena walked closer to Patrick and started kissing him continually.

"Stop, stop Elena, what are you doing?" he said.

Without any response from Elena. She continued, and they eventually made love inside the empty mill.

"Elena, we could have waited," said Patrick.

"Waited? For how long? My parents are against us being together. They will never accept our relationship," Elena said with tears in her eyes, and she continued to say, "It hurt me to say this to you right now but Patrick, you and I are never going to work. I am sorry, let us end it here," Elena said.

"End it? What do you mean? I promised to work hard. I will work hard; Elena please do not do this to us," Patrick said in a quavering voice.

"Please, please, I beg you, Elena. please do not do this, please Elena, I will work hard, let us not give up," he said.

"I cannot. I am sorry." Elena rushed out without saying any more words.

"Please don't go," he said softly while he continued to cry.

Elena! He yelled aloud one last time, but Elena was far gone.

## *CHAPTER THREE*

Weeks after Elena and Patrick left each other. Elena started to feel sick, so her mother went with her to visit their family doctor. When the result came out, the doctor delivered the result to them, and he went ahead to congratulate Elena on her pregnancy.

"Pregnant, who is pregnant? Elena, are you pregnant?" Mrs Gilbert asked.

"Mother, you heard the doctor. Yes, I am pregnant, and Patrick is the father," she replied.

"Oh my God. Elena, you have succeeded in bringing disgrace to our family," her mother said in anger. but Elena was not worried. She and her mother arrived home and the news about the pregnancy was brought to Mr Gilbert.

"Elena!" Mr Gilbert called out.

"Yes father, you called."

"What have you done Elena? You finally brought shame to the Gilbert's name. Elena, you have disgraced us, what will people say? How can I speak in public after this embarrassment that you have brought upon us?" Mr Gilbert said furiously.

"Father, you caused it. If you had allowed me to marry the man I love, this would not have happened."

"Shut up Elena, you are to leave this house at once and for this embarrassment that you have put in our name. You no longer have inheritance in this family. You shall take care of the child yourself, and no one in this family will support you," Mr Gilbert said in anger.

"Please darling. do not say that. She does not have anywhere to go. we cannot abandon her; she is our only daughter." Mrs Gilbert said.

"If you support or help her in any way, then you shall be next to leave this house."

Elena's brothers tried to intervene, but her father did not change his mind.

"This is cruel," Elena said as she walked away from them.

She took her belongings and went straight to Kate's. She told Kate what her father said after finding out she was pregnant.

"Elena, what should we do? You have no relatives here; you should tell Patrick, he is the father, and he has to be in the baby's life. I will go with you."

"No, I cannot. I broke up with him a few weeks ago, and I have not seen him since then."

"But he has to know," Kate said.

"I will take care of my baby myself; I have some savings," said Elena.

"Okay, you can stay with me for now. I will talk to my parents, and I also have little savings; I will give it to you, and we will take care of the child together. Do not worry, Elena."

"Thank you, Kate. What would I have done without you," Elena said as she gave Kate a warm hug.

A few days later, after much thought, Elena decided to find Patrick; she wanted him to know that she was carrying his child. While Elena and Kate were on their way, Elena said,

"I do not know his house. I have never been there."

"Okay, that's fine. We can just ask around when we arrive in his town," said Kate.

When they arrived in Patrick's town, they started to ask around and most people they asked didn't even know Patrick.

"I am tired already; we have been asking around and no one knows him. I think we should go back," Elena said.

"Are you sure he is from this town?" Kate asked.

"Yes, I think so," she replied. They were about to turn back when they saw an old man riding a bicycle towards them.

"Excuse me sir, excuse me. Do you know anybody called Patrick in this town? We have been asking around and no one knows him.

"Hmm Patrick, the tall one. Ah... yes, he is my neighbour. He lives with his mother but for several days now, I have not seen him around," the old man said.

"Do you see the compound with the flowers by the left?"

"Yes."

"That is where he lives."

"Thank you very much sir, we appreciate it," they said and continued to walk in the direction of the flowers.

"Hold on, young ladies." Elena and Kate stopped and looked at the old man.

"You look so much like a man I used to know," the old man said.

"Me?" Kate asked, as she points a finger to herself.

"No, not you. The fair one," the old man said as he pointed his finger to Elena.

"Oh me, really? Who was he?" Elena asked curiously.

"A young man I met over twenty-three years ago. He gave our town clean water by making us a borehole. He was a visionary and a very ambitious man. A year after he gave us clean water, we never saw him again," the old man said.

"He was indeed a good man; do you remember his name?" Elena asked.

"He asked us to call him Charlie and we all did but no one knew if it was his real name."

"I do not know anyone by that name," Elena said.

"Oh okay... anyway you should get going. Do not forget, the compound with the flowers," the old man said. They thanked him again and continued walking. "I know he was not talking about my father. My father would never help the town, unless he is getting something back in return. He only cares about the family's name and wealth," said Elena.

"And you do not resemble your father," said Kate. They arrived at the compound and Elena knocked on the front door.

"Who's there?" Patrick's mother asked as she stood up from the chair to open the door.

"How may I help you?"

"Hello ma, please, is Patrick around?" Elena asked.

"No, he travelled. and he will not be back anytime soon."

"Ah okay," Elena replied as she looked at Kate.

"Who are you, if I may ask."

"We are his friends from the neighbouring town. Please, whenever he returns, kindly tell him that Elena came looking for him."

"Okay, I will." They left Patrick's town and on their way home, Kate said,

"Why didn't you tell her that you are with Patrick's child?"

"I could not. I saw how she lives; she cannot support us. I will take care of my child myself, and besides, we have you," Elena said teasingly.

While Elena was pregnant, she got a part-time job delivering newspapers, in order to save more money. And some months later Elena gave birth to a baby girl and named her Irene. A year after she gave birth, Elena opened a pub right across her house in the centre of the town with her savings and the money she got from her friend Kate. She supported herself and her baby with whatever profit she made from her pub, and when Irene came of age, she began to help in running the pub.

## *CHAPTER FOUR*

After a long day on the farm, Mr Ryan returned home and decided to take a nap. A few minutes later the telephone began to ring continuously.

*Driiin!*

He sat up and after a couple seconds he walked up to the telephone stand behind his television shelf.

"Hello," he said.

"Hello, is this Mr Ryan?" the stranger asked.

"Yes, who is this?"

"I am Sir William; you made an inquiry into buying my plots of land, the one besides the cashew farm. I was informed that you rear animals, and you are not from my town."

"Ah yes, I am interested in purchasing your land sir, and yes, I rear livestock and I intend to extend my farm, and I think the land will be good for farming.

"Okay, so let me know when you are free so I can show you around. And if you are still interested, we can talk about the prize," said Sir William.

"Alright, will tomorrow at noon be okay?"

"Yes, let's meet at the town hall tomorrow by noon."

"Okay sir."

The next day Mr Ryan got dressed, brought out his motorcycle and headed to the appointment in the next town. When he and Sir William were done surveying the land, they fixed another appointment to settle the payment of the land. Sir William entered his car and drove away, while Mr Ryan got on his motorcycle and started riding home. Then it suddenly began to rain heavily, so he came across a pub in the centre of the town, parked his motorcycle and walked inside. His jacket was soaked with water. He took off his jacket and hung it on a wooden stand behind the door.

"Excuse me, can I have a bottle of beer," he said as he walked in and sat by the window in the last row.

"Bottle of beer..., coming right up," Elena said as she hurried her way to the fridge and took a bottle of beer and a glass cup from the shelf.

"Here it is sir," she said.

"Thank you," Mr Ryan replied.

Elena was the only one working at the pub that day, Irene had gone for her music class.

Mr Ryan poured a tangible amount of beer into the glass cup and took a big sip while he waits for the rain to stop. Mr Ryan being the only customer in the pub on that rainy day, Elena started a conversation with him.

"There weren't any weather updates that it was going to rain today," she said right from the counter.

"Yes, I am surprised it's raining so heavily," said Mr Ryan.

"You are not from around here," she said.

"What makes you say so?"

"I know almost everybody from this town; it's a small town and I run the only pub here," said Elena.

"Yes, you are right, I am from the neighbouring town. I am here to purchase land for farming."

"Oh, that's nice, have you seen any land that you are interested in?" she said.

"Yes, I like the land beside the cashew farm, and I just had a meeting with the owner."

"That is great. What type of farm if I may ask? she said curiously.

"Livestock. I rear sheep and pigs."

"That's interesting," Elena said.

So, it finally stopped raining. Mr Ryan paid for his beer, took his jacket and was about to head out, when Elena said,

"You can always visit our pub whenever you're in town."

"Sure, I will. Ms...?" he said, waiting for her to complete his sentence with her name.

"Elena, my name is Elena," she said while smiling.

Mr Ryan returned home, a week later he finalised and paid for the plots of land. While he was constructing the ranches in his new land, Mr Ryan visited Elena's pub all the time; they soon became friends and Mr

Ryan got to meet Irene, Elena's daughter. One evening Mr Ryan was in Elena's pub as usual, when Irene walked in. She looked incredibly sad like she had been crying; when Elena saw her daughter and how she looked she began to worry. Without hesitation she took Irene to the storage room to ask what the problem was.

"What happened? Why do you look so sad?"

"Mother, I don't think I will attend the music class anymore," Irene said angrily.

What happened, dear? But I already paid the fees," Elena said as she held Irene's hand.

"I got bullied today; someone called me a bastard. I was hurt." Irene burst out crying.

Elena drew closer to her and wiped off the tears in her eyes and said,

"You are not a bastard. You have a father, and you will meet him someday."

"But when, mother," Irene said angrily.

"Irene my dear girl, I promise you, you will meet him," Elena said. and she gave Irene a hug.

"Mother, I want to go home and rest. I will come back in the evening to help."

"Yes dear, go home, eat and rest."

As Irene walked out from the pub, Mr Ryan was curious, he wanted to know why Irene looked sad. So, he waited for Elena to return from the storage room some minutes later. And he asked, "Is everything all right with the little one? She did not look too good today."

"Nothing serious, she just had a tough day at school. She was bullied by her classmate."

"Oh, now I understand. It will get better; some younger people are very mean. They talk without thinking," Mr Ryan said while sipping from his glass of beer.

"I hope it will get better. she is going through a lot, and it is my fault that she is being bullied."

"Your fault? How?"

Elena walked closer and sat next to Mr Ryan. "You see... I was engaged once. His name was Patrick, and he held my heart, but he was a carpenter. I loved him, but my family was against our relationship. They wanted a rich son-in-law. It was either Patrick or my family. I had to give up both, because I wanted peace. But soon after I left Patrick, I found out I was pregnant. That did not sit well with my father, so he sent me out from the house for bringing disgrace to the family."

"Oh my god. It must have been really hard for you."

"Yes, it was. But I have a friend who supported me throughout."

"You have done an amazing job raising your daughter. Look at her... beautiful and very smart."

After she told Mr Ryan about all she has been through, Mr Ryan told her about his own story. About how he was married to a woman who never loved him.

Weeks later, Mr Ryan finished constructing his ranch. He purchased some livestock and employed workers in it. He visited his farm every last day of the week and before he returns home, he would always visit Elena and her daughter. Mr Ryan began developing interest in Elena. Whenever he comes visiting, he always buys Elena a basket of fruits and sometimes a book. After a short while, Mr Ryan began to court Elena. On one particular week. Mr Ryan went to his farm as usual and visited Elena and her daughter, while they were all in the pub talking and laughing.

"Next Saturday is my birthday, and I would like you to come and celebrate with me. My childhood friend is visiting as well. So, I would like you to meet him," said Mr Ryan.

"Of course. I will be there," Elena replied.

"Mother, can I go with you?" said Irene.

"No dear, if we both attend the party, who will run the pub that day?"

"Oh yes, that's true, don't worry Mr Ryan, I will send my gift."

"Hahaha, thank you. That is truly kind of you."

That evening after Mr Ryan had left, Irene said to her mother.,

"I see you like Mr Ryan and I think he likes you too. Would you marry him?"

"Marry? What do you mean? You are my priority right now. I might like Mr Ryan, but I like you more," Elena answered.

"Mother, for 18 years you have been taking care of me alone, you should be happy. This time take care of yourself, if you want to marry him, I give you my blessing."

"Thank you for saying that, but Mr Ryan hasn't asked me to marry him yet."

"I know he will. He like you very much and I like him," Irene said.

## *CHAPTER FIVE*

Mr Ryan's birthday came so fast, and Elena was looking forward to it. That Saturday Elena prepared a birthday present, and she wore a beautiful blue dress and a matching hat that Kate had made specially for her. Elena looked gorgeous as she gets ready to step out from the house.

"Mother, mother, wait. I prepared a present for Mr Ryan," said Irene as she hurried inside to bring out the gift.

"Okay, I'm waiting."

"Here it is, wow mother... you look stunning. I have never seen you look this beautiful," said Irene.

"Thank you. I did not know that I still have this spark in me," she said while smiling.

"Mother, have fun."

"Yes, I will," she replied, and they said goodbye as she rode her bicycle away.

Thirty-five minutes later, Elena arrived at Mr Ryan's town. The town looked really familiar to her; the moment she rode past the flowers that were in front of Patrick's house, was when she remembered the first time, she ever visited the town. But Elena did not stop to ask about Patrick, she rode past, even though the wooden door was half open. Some minutes later, she got to Mr Ryan's house, and she was invited in.

"You look beautiful and thank you for coming," said Mr Ryan.

"Thank you... and happy birthday," Elena said while she blushes, and she handed him the gifts she brought. Mr Ryan took Elena to a particular side and offered her a glass of wine and a chair to sit on.

"I will be right back, I need to get more drinks, please feel comfortable," he said as he walked out the front door while the music "elements of vogue by DePino" was playing in the background. All the guests were choosing a partner to dance with. Elena sat calmly as she watches the people who were dancing. A man came from behind and he said, "Would you do me the honour?" and he stretched forth his right hand. Elena hesitated when she looked up and saw the face of the man. She was in disbelief. The man asked again. "Would you do me the honour?" whilst still stretching forth his hand.

"Yes," Elena replied and took his hand, and they began dancing.

"You look beautiful," he said as their hands were wrapped around each other.

"Thank you, you look great too."

"We never had the chance to dance like this, when we were younger."

"Yes, I know."

"How have you been Elena?"

"Better. I have been better..."

"Did you marry a rich man?" he asked, and for a split moment they stopped dancing before continuing again.

"No. I never got the chance. I was busy taking care of my responsibility."

"Giving us up did not take a lot. You hurt me, Elena."

"Stop, Patrick." Elena yelled aloud. "You did not know the choice I had to make. It was either you or my family and I chose none. I was exhausted and the mess was too much for me to handle. I was tired Patrick; I was tired," Elena said as she was about to walk away from Patrick. Mr Ryan entered and walked towards them and said. "Oh. I see you have met my childhood friend Patrick. Patrick, this is Elena, the woman after my heart." Elena and Patrick were both silent for a moment before they said hello.

"She is a beautiful woman," Patrick said.

"Yes, she is," Mr Ryan replied.

Elena and Patrick sat awkwardly without saying anything to each other. Elena then stood up and took a stroll outside as the weather was warm and enjoyable. A few minutes later Mr Ryan joined Elena and they started to chat.

"I really enjoyed myself today. Thanks for inviting me," she said.

"You're welcome." He held Elena's hand and he continued to say, "I am falling in love with you Elena.

There is something about you that I cannot get enough of."

"Wait... you might not want me after this."

"What, how do you mean? I will always want you."

"Your friend and I had a past; he is the Patrick I told you about, the carpenter."

"Wait, this Patrick? He is Irene's father? And he does not know?" Mr Ryan said in shock.

"No, and I do not intend to tell him. I have taken good care of Irene for 18 years; we do not need him."

"You must let him know. He has no idea that he has a child with you. Please Elena, tell him. Do not take this away from Irene. She has to know her father. Do not take this opportunity away from her, she deserves to know.

"Okay, I will tell him, but only when I am ready."

"Are you still in love with him?" Mr Ryan asked.

"No, 18 years is a long time, and he should be married by now, you look worried."

"Yes, I am a little bit scared."

"You do not have to be. I care about you, and I want us to work. Irene likes you."

"Really?" he said happily.

"Yes, she even gave us her blessing, she asked me to be happy."

"You deserve it, you should be happy." So, they talked for a bit more and it was time for Elena to go home because it was getting late. "Before you leave, would you dance with me?" he said.

"Yes, I would love to." Mr Ryan and Elena danced and enjoyed the evening before she left.
Mr Ryan pretended he did not know about Patrick and Elena's past. As he and Patrick drank and talked about their old days, Patrick never said anything about Elena to Mr Ryan. They jollied, and after the celebration was over, all the guests returned to their various homes.

When Elena arrived home that evening, she could not bring herself to tell her daughter that she saw her father. She kept it to herself, thinking about how she was going to explain why Patrick was not in Irene's life. Some days later, when she and Irene were done eating dinner, she said silently to Irene,

"Haven't I been a good mother to you?"

"Of course, you have, is anything the matter? Did I offend you, mother?"

"No dear, do you really need a father?"
Irene became curious as she put down the cup of water she was holding and said, "Yes, I need a father and I want to know about my father."

"But why? I am your father and your mother as well," said Elena.

"I know you have played the role of a father all these years but tell me, is my father still alive? Where is he from or did he abandon us? Is that why you do not talk about him?" said Irene.

"Your father is alive and well and as a matter of fact I saw him a few days ago at Mr Ryan's birthday."

Elena started crying and continued saying, "It is all my fault. I was scared and so I broke his heart. I thought I was doing the right thing and still today he does not know he has a child with me. I went looking for him after your aunt Kate persuaded me, but he had left town. I did not tell his family; I am so sorry Irene. Everything you went through is all my fault."

Irene kept quiet for some time after hearing everything her mother said.

"You said you saw him a few days ago? Why didn't you tell him about me? Mother, it has been 18 years, how can you do this to me and him? Why mother?"

Irene could not hold back her tears. When she was done blaming her mother, she left the house angrily. Elena sat quietly at the dining table, realising all the pain she has caused her daughter.

The next morning Elena went to Mr Ryan's house unannounced.

"Elena... why are you here this early? Is everything okay? Is Irene okay? He said anxiously.

"Irene is not okay, I told her about Patrick, she's hurt, I hurt her," she responded.

Mr Ryan opened the door widely and took Elena inside, he then gave Elena his handkerchief that was on top of his table. "Take, wipe your tears, I can tell it did not go well, stop blaming yourself, you have a chance now to make everything right. I have known Patrick for a very long time; he did not have a father and he went through a lot as well. He had a difficult childhood and I know he would not wish that for his own child. Elena... let them meet," Mr Ryan said.

"Can you help me arrange a meeting with Patrick today or has he left town?"

He is still around, and of course we can go to his house later, if you want, so you can tell him everything. When the day got brighter, Mr Ryan accompanied Elena to Patrick's house. When Patrick saw Elena and Mr Ryan that morning, he was surprised and after they exchanged greetings, he said.

"Come in and have a seat, to what do I owe this visit?"

Mr Ryan looked at Elena and said,

"We have a very important thing to tell you." Patrick became curious.

"Important? Are you getting married? Patrick said teasingly, and they all laughed.

Mr Ryan held Elena's hand and asked her to go ahead.

"A few weeks after we went our separate ways, I started feeling sick and visited the doctor and the result came back that I was pregnant," said Elena.

Patrick became confused and said,

"Pregnant, you were pregnant?"

"Yes Patrick, I was pregnant."

"Why didn't you reach out to me?"

"I did. I visited your home and met your mother, and she told me you travelled and will not be back in a long time, so I never bothered to tell her about the pregnancy."

"Elena, you mean I have a child with you?" he asked in excitement, and he turned to Mr Ryan and said. "You knew about Elena and I, but you never said anything,"

"Yes, Elena told me everything, and it is in the past now"

"Yes, it is," and Patrick turned and said to Elena, "I am sorry, my mother never told me, I think she forgot, her sickness worsened after I left."

"Oh... sorry, I did not know that. And yes, we have a child Patrick, and her name is Irene. She is smart and... beautiful," Elena said as tears rolled down from her eyes. "And she wants to meet you."

"Oh my god, when can I see her? It has been 18 years. I missed out on a lot, but what did your family say after they found out?"

"I was sent out from the house," Elena replied.

"What? How can they do that to their own child?" Patrick said angrily.

"My family only cares about riches and they are willing to do anything to increase their wealth."

"You see, when you left me in that mill, broken and hurt, I managed to return home after several hours, but I was not myself for days. I thought about a lot of things; I blamed my mother for giving birth to me, I blamed God for making us poor. And a few days later I got an opportunity to travel to England to work as a manservant in exchange for a tuition fee. I did not mind serving for 6 years, I studied, and, in a few years, I graduated and became an architect. Two years later,

I met an English woman, whom I married, and she bore me a son. Now, I own lots of properties… I own lands, Elena." Patrick started sobbing.

"I have always wished you well and I am glad that you prospered," Elena said.

"This is no time to talk about the past, you should meet her and make up for all those years you missed in her life," said Mr Ryan.

Patrick wiped off the tears on his eyes, and he asked again, "Please, when can I see my daughter?"

"On Saturday, she doesn't attend her music class on Saturdays," said Elena.

"Okay then, I will come but where?"

"To my home, in the next town, opposite the pub I run, in the centre of the town. Come by noon."

After they finished talking and fixed a date to meet, Elena returned home and told her daughter that her father was coming to meet her on Saturday of that week. Irene was excited, and she apologised to her mother for all the harsh words she said.

## *CHAPTER SIX*

Heavy music was coming out from the Gilbert's house. Henry walked in and saw a lot of people drinking and whoring in the hall.

"Brother, what is all this? Send them away this instant before father returns."

"Why would I do that? I am having fun. Come join us, and besides, father has gone to see his mistress as usual," said Erik.

"Stop it. Do not say that, there are people here."

"Are you ashamed? I am speaking the truth. He sent Elena out of the family and now he is hurting mother emotionally."

"Stop brother, stop talking nonsense," said Henry as he tried collecting the cup of alcohol from his brother.

"Stop? Are you not tired of being used by father? I am tired. Elena was the only person who challenged him."

"And see where it led her, we are only related in the family registry. She has no inheritance from father, we all saw how she suffered to care for her bastard child and look how she has grown so old. When she was here, she had fine clothes, lots of jewellery and nice shoes. I do not wish to be like her."

"But she was different from us. She spoke. She challenged father. I just wish I could live my life without father interfering," Erik said angrily.

"You enjoy riches, father bought properties in our names, and we should be grateful."

"Grateful, you say. Properties at the expense of our freedom and happiness. I am tired Henry; I do not want to continue living like this."

Henry burst out laughing. "You do not want? You make me laugh, don't you think it is too late..., with those grey hairs on your head," Henry said.

"Father has destroyed us, he made us like this."

"You are drunk, come brother..." he reaches for Erik's arm. "I will retire you to your bed."

"Let go of me!" Erik yelled out. Henry held him tightly and started taking him away from the hall. "Watch your step big brother." He guided Erik to his room and put him in bed.

"There... you go. Isn't the bed warm and comfy?" Henry said. He then went to the hall and sent all the guests away.

The next morning, Erik went to the dining room to have his breakfast, and he met Henry and their mother eating.

"How's your hangover?" Henry asked.

"Ahh... my head still hurts." As he took a sip from his tea, he looked at Henry and said,

"Brother, forget about everything I said last night, I was drunk."

"Yes. Of course, I will not bring it up."

"Bring what up, did something happen last night while I was at my cousin's? Mrs Gilbert asked.

"No mother," they both said.

It was Friday and Elena was already anticipating the next day. which was the day Patrick would come. The Saturday came and she was anxious.

"Are you okay, mother?" Irene asked.

"Yes dear, I am okay." she said.

"Look mother, it's almost noon," said Irene as she pointed to the clock.

A few minutes later, they heard a knock on the door. Elena stood up from where she was sitting and opened the door. Patrick was standing while he held a bunch of flowers, and before Patrick entered inside the house, Irene felt nervous and went straight into her room.

"You're here, come in," said Elena as she led him to a place to sit.

"Thank you, your home is beautiful," said Patrick.

Patrick sat down and he was offered a glass of gin. "Irene!" Elena called out.

"But she was just here, where did she go?" she said and walked directly to Irene's room.

"There you are, he is here, your father is here."

"Mother, I am nervous," Irene said as she walked closer to her mother.

"Oh, my sweet girl, don't be." Elena gave her a little pep talk and a few minutes later, they both came out from the room and walked to where Patrick was sitting.

"This is Irene, our daughter. Irene meet Patrick, your father," Elena said. Patrick stood up immediately and gave Irene a hug.

"She is beautiful," he said, and he handed Irene the flowers he brought. They both said hello and Elena felt so relieved as she looked at both of them talking and smiling. They chatted for some hours, and Patrick invited Irene to his place so she can meet the rest of the family. Irene was happy, she finally felt like she belonged somewhere. It has always been her and her mother all those years. Before Patrick left, he thanked Elena for taking good care of their daughter alone for 18 years.

Patrick built a relationship with his daughter and tried making up for all the years he missed. A few months later Mr Ryan married Elena, and Irene became his stepdaughter. Irene moved to England with her father and continued her studies over there.

Three years later, Mr Ryan became sick with cancer and was admitted to the hospital. While he was fighting for his life, the Gilberts tried to walk their way back into Elena's life, seeing how Elena's life changed after she married Mr Ryan and knowing that Elena was unable to give Mr Ryan a child. One evening when Elena was getting ready to go visit Mr Ryan in the hospital, a car drove into their compound, and Elena looked through the window to see who it was. She saw her father come out from the car and was coming towards the front door. She waited patiently for him to get to the door. He was about to knock before Elena spoke loudly.

"What is it, father?" She collected her purse from the table and opened the door.

"Elena, is this how you greet your old father?" said Mr Gilbert.

"What do you want, father? I am heading out, as you can see," said Elena as she began to lock the front door.

"I hear Mr Ryan is sick, he has cancer. Will he make it?"

"Father, do you wish him dead? He is my husband, and I will appreciate it if you do not speak ill of him."

"Your husband, I never gave him my blessing. I am still your father, and we are still family."

"Stop. you sent me away and gave me no inheritance. Kate, Irene, and Mr Ryan are my only family," Elena said furiously, and she walked away leaving her father behind.

When Elena got to the hospital, she saw Mr Ryan crying, and she hurried towards his bed and held his hand

"Darling, what is it?" she said.

"I am tired of fighting, I want to give up now," he said as he continued to cry.

"Do not say that. I know you can do it, please do not leave us," Elena said.

"Listen to me Elena, I spoke with my lawyer this morning. I have willed all my properties to you, whatever I have is now yours and Irene's."

Elena began crying.

"I do not need properties; it is you I need. Promise me you will keep fighting; promise me you will not give up."

As they were still talking, Elena's brothers walked in. Elena stood up immediately as she saw them.

"What do the Gilberts want again? Get out," Elena yelled out.

"Stop yelling and hear us out. Mother is here at the hospital, she's sick Elena," Henry said.

"How is that my business, am I your family?" Elena asked.

"Yes, we are your family, and nothing can change that."

"You all saw me suffer and none of you offered me help, even mother, and you say we are family. This is my family here." She pointed to Mr Ryan.

"You call this dying man your family? I pity you, Elena. Father is already interested in Mr Ryan's properties; Mr Ryan does not have an heir and Irene cannot put claims to his properties. Elena...your name is still in the Gilbert family registry, or did you forget?" said Henry.

Elena got terribly angry after hearing what her brother said. So, she continued to yell out.

"Get out, get out, I said get out of this room."

Her brothers got scared and were leaving the room when Erik said,

"I am sorry Elena, I couldn't do anything, I am deeply sorry."

"I hate you all!" Elena said, as tears dropped down her eyes.

"Come Elena, come sit close to me," said Mr Ryan. Elena went and sat by his bedside.

"Stop crying, it hurts me to see you cry." He used his hand to wipe off the tears on Elena's face.

"If I had given you a child, my family would not be fighting over properties that they do not own. They even lied about mother being sick just to come here," said Elena.

"You and Irene are all that I need," said Mr Ryan.

Elena returned home that evening feeling sad. She thought about everything her family said and after some time she telephoned Kate and told her everything and Kate assured her that everything will be okay, and that she should not give up hope on Mr Ryan. When she was done talking to Kate, she fell asleep on the couch. The next morning, Mr Ryan had a visit from his ex-wife.

"Hello..." Anna said as she walked into the hospital room that Mr Ryan was.

"Oh hi, come in and have a seat."

"I heard you were sick," Anna said and tried explaining how she heard.

"You know it's a small town and they talk, but how are you feeling?"

"Yeah, I know our town and how they talk, but er... I am fine. I am still fighting and hoping to beat cancer. But how is your family?"

"I am sure you will beat it; you are a strong man. And my family is fine," she said.

"Thank you for saying that" Mr Ryan said. After Anna stayed and talked with Mr Ryan for some time and then she got up from the chair and said goodbye and she headed out. On her way, she kept thinking to herself how Mr Ryan was a good man and she regretted not knowing who he really is before she left him.

After some months, Mr Ryan won the battle with cancer, and he became healthy. Soon after he resumed working. The Gilberts were not happy about the news of Mr Ryan's health. So, Elena took the Gilberts to court.

"Court... stand." The court clerk said aloud as the judge came in. The judge listened to Elena and Mr Gilbert and made a ruling, that the Gilberts should stay away from Elena and asked her name to be removed from the family registry only if Elena requested it to be removed. When Elena got home, she called her husband in excitement...

"Darling, darling! where are you?"

"I am here," Mr Ryan responded from the backyard. Elena walked to the backyard and said in excitement, "Alas. I am free from the Gilberts, and I shall have my name removed from the family registry."

"Wow. This is a call for celebration," said Mr Ryan. And he moved closer to Elena.

"Darling. Is this what you truly want?"

"I do not understand what you mean," Elena replied.

"I mean, do you really want to forget about your family? They might be money-driven but they are still your family."

"What should I do? I do not wish to get involved with them anymore."

"Do whatever you wish to do, and I will stand by you." A few moments later, after she gave it some thought.

"Okay, I shall hold on from removing my name from the family registry. It is not what I truly want but they have hurt me too much."

"I know my darling. But you cannot change the past."

"You are right. I cannot change the past. I shall hold on; else I be a woman with no lineage.

After the court, Elena and Mr Ryan lived harmoniously for two seasons. One Sunday evening, Elena and Mr Ryan returned home from the town gathering.

"Oh... we are finally home; the meeting was chaotic today," said Elena.

"Yes, it was. Did you notice that the alderman was a bit drunk today? He was talking gibberish. Every word he said made no sense," said Mr Ryan and they burst out laughing.

"Yes. It was funny listening to him,"

Elena replied as they continued to laugh. And when they walked to the front door, Elena placed in the key to open the door, then she noticed a brown envelope underneath the door. She bent down and collected it.

"Oh, it's a letter... with the Gilbert's seal,"

said Elena, and she showed it to Mr Ryan.

"What do you think they want this time?" she said.

"Come on. I am sure it is nothing. We will read it together after we have had supper," Mr Ryan replied.

That same evening after they had supper, Elena brought out the letter with Mr Ryan sitting across from her at the table. Elena took a deep breath and said quietly,

"It's only a letter." She took a long glance at the seal and then opened the letter and began to read.

*Dear Elena,*

*Hope you are well? I know that you are wondering why I wrote this letter. I will go straight to the point; I am getting old, and time is no*

*more on my side, but I know that you do not care if I live or die. When I sent you out from the house, I wanted to reach out to you so many times, it broke my heart watching you suffer but my pride did not allow me to bring you back in or offer to help so I protected and helped you from afar. You might be thinking. "What help and protection is he talking about?" from the place you stayed while you were pregnant to the gifts you received at the hospital. I did all that. Do not blame Kate and her family. I made her parents swear not to tell you. Did you think that they would have allowed you to live in their house and eat their food for over a year without contributing. I know you are disappointed. But even if I had the courage years ago and offered to help, would you have accepted? I and the other Gilberts have hurt you, but it will gladden my heart if you could find a place in your heart to forgive us. And another reason I am writing this letter is to inform you that I cannot remove your name from the Gilbert family registry. Because my late brother Charles and his wife Magdalene, will never forgive me from their grave. ELENA, YOU ARE A GILBERT AND ALWAYS WILL BE.*

*Father*

After she finished reading the letter, Elena was left confused with how the letter ended. The evening of the next day Elena and Mr Ryan pay a visit to the Gilberts.

"I was expecting you but not this soon," said Mr Gilbert.

"You knew I'd come here, didn't you?" said Elena.

"Of course, but before we continue talking, I want your mother and your brothers here with us," said Mr Gilbert and he called the rest of the family to the living room. A few minutes later, Mrs Gilbert, Erik and Henry walked in and before they sat down Mrs Gilbert said,

"Oh Elena, welcome, it's been so long, how is your daughter?"

"My daughter is doing well, thank you for asking."

"Father, can we talk now, what do you mean by your brother Charles and Magdalene will never forgive you?"

Mr Gilbert looked at his wife and hesitated for some seconds before he replied.

"I knew this day would come."

"Go on darling, it's been too long."

"Elena, my brother Charles, made this family what we are today. At a very young age he travelled abroad, and when he returned after five years, he was a changed man, and with the little fortune he brought, he invested it in lands and waited for some years before reselling them. He made more than ten times the money he invested but he did not stop there; he built this house and invited our father and I to live with him. He bought every property we own today; he even went to the neighbouring town and gave them clean water," said Mr Gilbert.

"Did you say he gave the neighbouring town clean water? Father did people call him Charlie? said Elena as she immediately remembered what the old man said to her years ago.

"Yes, but how did you know that people called him Charlie?"

"I met an old man years ago, who told me about Charlie; he said I looked like him, but I never knew that I was related to him."

"Yes, you resemble him in every way," Mr Gilbert replied.

"But how come you never told us anything about him?" Erik asked.

"Because he met an unfortunate end, and our father forbade us from talking about it before he passed."

"But father, why?" Elena replied. Mr Gilbert sighed deeply and continued saying.

"Charles met Magdalene the blacksmith's daughter and he wanted to marry her. But our father was against it; at that time, we were already among the wealthiest families in this town. So, Charles moved out from the house and moved in with Magdalene and her father. And they had a daughter. Two months later, we received news that there was a fire outbreak in the blacksmith's house and there were no survivors except the baby that was placed on the ground outside the burning house. An eyewitness said that it was Charles who brought out the baby and he rushed back inside but he never made it out again."

"Oh my God, where is that baby now?" said Henry.

"Here, with us?"

"Father, what do you mean?" said henry.

"That baby was you, Elena. I took you in as my own."

When Mr Gilbert said that everybody was shocked. And the living room was silent for a moment.

"You see why I cannot remove your name from the Gilberts, even if you requested it. Your mother and I swore to take this secret to the grave, but you were just like your father Charles."

Elena started to cry.

"Darling, wipe your tears," Mr Ryan said quietly as he handed her his handkerchief.

"We are sorry Elena, for sending you out of your own father's house. Forgive us," said Mrs Gilbert.

Mr Gilbert sighed quietly and said,

"I think, I am being punished by the heavens for being too greedy. Elena, please forgive us, I have arranged every document of your inheritance. I will give them to you now."

Mr Gilbert went inside his room and brought out some papers and handed them to Elena.

"These are the documents of every property your father owns, including this house. Elena exhaled slowly and collected the papers.

"Father, where would we go if Elena takes this house?" said Henry but Mr Gilbert did not respond.

"Despite everything I have heard today, you are both my parents. You raised me, so I cannot send you out from the only home you have known; you may continue to live here for the rest of your days. And I thank you for taking me in and for every help you gave me when I was away. I forgive you all. After all we are family, we are the Gilberts, Elena said.

"Thank you, thank you Elena. Now I am free from the secret I have carried for so long. Thank you, daughter," said Mr Gilbert.

"Let's share wine for this wonderful reunion," said Mrs Gilbert as she hurried to bring a bottle of red wine and some glass cups. Henry poured wine into all the glass cups and said,

"To the Gilberts." And they all raised their glasses and said, "TO THE GILBERTS!"

From that day forward, Elena and her family united and her friend Kate apologised on behalf of her parents. And they all lived in HARMONY.

www.ingramcontent.com/pod-product-compliance
Lightning Source LLC
La Vergne TN
LVHW090136160826
845673LV00017B/2494

* 9 7 9 8 3 5 7 6 9 3 9 5 2 *